R0061363230

12/2011

D1368792

Dear mouse friends,
Welcome to the world of

Geronimo Stilton

The Editorial Staff of
The Rodent's Gazette

1. Linda Thinslice
2. Sweetie Cheesetriangle
3. Ratella Redfur
4. Soya Mousehao
5. Cheesita de la Pampa
6. Coco Chocamouse
7. Mouseanna Mousetti
8. Patty Plumprat
9. Tina Spicytail
10. William Shortpaws
11. Valerie Vole
12. Trap Stilton
13. Dolly Fastpaws
14. Zeppola Zap
15. Merenguita Gingermouse
16. Shorty Tao
17. Baby Tao
18. Gigi Gogo
19. Teddy von Muffler
20. Thea Stilton
21. Erronea Misprint
22. Pinky Pick
23. Ya-ya O'Cheddar
24. Ratsy O'Shea
25. Geronimo Stilton
26. Benjamin Stilton
27. Briette Finerat
28. Raclette Finerat
29. Mousella MacMouser
30. Kreamy O'Cheddar
31. Blasco Tabasco
32. Toffie Sugarsweet
33. Tylerat Truemouse
34. Larry Keys
35. Michael Mouse

Geronimo Stilton
A learned and brainy
mouse; editor of
The Rodent's Gazette

Thea Stilton
Geronimo's sister and
special correspondent at
The Rodent's Gazette

Trap Stilton
An awful joker;
Geronimo's cousin and
owner of the store
Cheap Junk for Less

Benjamin Stilton
A sweet and loving
nine-year-old mouse;
Geronimo's favorite
nephew

Geronimo Stilton

THE SECRET OF CACKLEFUR CASTLE

Scholastic Inc.

New York   Toronto   London   Auckland   Sydney

Mexico City   New Delhi   Hong Kong   Buenos Aires

ISBN-13: 978-0-439-69145-1
ISBN-10: 0-439-69145-1

Text by Geronimo Stilton
Original title: *Il segreto della famiglia Tenebrax*
Cover by Larry Keys
Illustrations Larry Keys, Blasco Tabasco, and Toffina Sakkarina
Graphics by Merenguita Gingermouse

Special thanks to Tracey West
Interior design by Kay Petronio

20 19 18 17 16   11 12/0

Printed in the U.S.A.   40
First printing, August 2005

ON A CHEESY AUTUMN AFTERNOON

Let me introduce myself. My name is Stilton, *Geronimo Stilton*. I run *The Rodent's Gazette,* the most *famouse* newspaper on Mouse Island. My office is in 17 Swiss Cheese Center.

That is where I was when this terrifying tale began. It was a beautiful **autumn** afternoon at the end of October.

"What a lovely, peaceful day!" I said out loud.

I spoke too soon. All of a

sudden, the walls started to shake.

Vrooooooooooom!

A loud roaring sound filled my office. My desk began to tremble. The pencil cup that my aunt Sweetfur gave me for my birthday tumbled to the floor.

"Holey cheese!" I cried.

vrooooooooo oo ooooooom!

The roaring got louder. Then a mouse on a motorcycle rode through my door. It was my sister, Thea, of course.

Thea Stilton

"Thea!" I squeaked. "How many times do I have to tell you not to ride your motorcycle into my office!"

"I'm worried about you, Geronimo," Thea said. "You have not written a new book in a long time. What's wrong?"

Thea is a special correspondent for *The Rodent's Gazette.* Still, I did not appreciate her sticking her snout into my business.

I pointed to the pile of papers on my desk. "I am too busy to *write*," I said. "There is lots of other work to do around here."

Thea frowned. "This is not like you, Geronimo. You always had time to write before!" she scolded. Then she peeled out of the office, her tires SQUEALING.

I sighed and sat down at my desk. What could I do? I had to do my paperwork.

My tail had just hit the chair when the

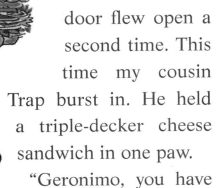

Trap Stilton

door flew open a second time. This time my cousin Trap burst in. He held a triple-decker cheese sandwich in one paw.

"Geronimo, you have become lazier than a mouse with an automatic cheese slicer. You must write something new!" he yelled.

"I need to be inspired before I can write," I huffed. "I can't just pluck an idea out of my whiskers."

The door flew open a third time. Pinky Pick, my very young assistant editor, bounded

Pinky Pick

in. "Hey, Boss!" she said cheerfully. "I am organizing a PARTY for your next book. It's going to be *fabumouse*!"

My tail twitched. I was starting to get annoyed. "But I haven't even written it yet!" I squeaked.

The door flew open a fourth time. It was my favorite nephew, Benjamin, on his way home from school. "Hello, Uncle," he said. "My friends are all asking when your next book is coming out!"

I felt embarrassed. I hated to disappoint Benjamin. He gazed up at me with his sweet round eyes. "It will be out soon, Benjamin," I said. "I promise."

Benjamin Stilton

Trap, Pinky, and Benjamin left me to my work. I finished

I looked out over New Mouse City.

the stack of papers on my desk. But I could not stop thinking about what everyone had said. What would my next book be about?

The beautiful autumn afternoon turned into a beautiful crisp evening. I looked outside my window and gazed out over **NEW MOUSE CITY**. A cold wind blew up and lifted the cheddar-colored leaves off the ground. **I watched them float and swirl in the night air.**

I needed an **idea**. But I didn't have any! I had to think. I sat down at my desk. . . .

A few hours later, I was still thinking.

I had no ideas. NOTHING. My mind was as dry as a stale slice of cheese.

Feeling helpless, I started to sob. "It is no use!" I moaned.

"My writing days are over!"

A Mysterious Phone Call

The phone rang, drowning out my sobs.

Riiiiing! Riiiiing! Riiiiing!

I wiped the tears off my whiskers. Then I picked up the phone.

"Hello," I said sadly. "Stilton speaking, *Geronimo Stilton*."

"Is that you, my little cheese nip?" a sickly sweet voice asked.

My fur stood on end. I knew that voice. It was **CREEPELLA VON CACKLEFUR!**

I first met Creepella last October. She is not like other mice. She has shiny gray fur. Her eyes are

sigh!

as **GREEN** as poisonous snakes. She wears a long purple gown and matching purple pawnail polish.

Creepella's father, Boris, lives in a funeral parlor at 33 Dark Grave Drive. Creepella lives in a crypt in the cemetery. Her mouse hole is filled with **COBWEBS** and **DEAD FLOWERS**.

All that is pretty spooky. But here is the scariest part of all: Creepella wants me to be her boyfriend!

"Hello, Creepella," I said nervously.

"I need you, Geronimo," Creepella said. "My grandfather Professor Frankenstein has died. His will is being read tomorrow night. I need to leave for CACKLEFUR CASTLE right away. It's in the Valley of the Vain VAMPIRES. I need you to come with me, my little bat wing."

Cacklefur Castle? The Valley of the Vain Vampires? I hate things that are spooky!

But Creepella was not finished yet. "It will be wonderful, Geronimo," she said. "I'll introduce you to my family."

Her family? I had already met her father, and he was creepy enough. I really did not want to meet any more Cacklefurs.

"I'm sorry, Creepella," I said quickly. "I can't go with you. I am busy...um... *working on my next book*!"

"Really?" Creepella asked. She sounded **suspicious**. "What is it about?"

I didn't know what to say. "Um...it's a secret!" I lied.

Creepella didn't buy it. "Your book can wait, my little toadstool. I will be at your office with my hearse faster than a spider can

CREEPELLA VON CACKLEFUR

Who Is She? She is a special effects designer for scary films and haunted houses. Her father is Boris von Cacklefur. Creepella is an enchanting and mysterious mouse with a pet bat named Bitewing.

Her Secret: She has a crush on Geronimo Stilton!

BORIS VON CACKLEFUR

Who Is He? He runs Fabumouse Funerals, a funeral home at 33 Dark Grave Drive. His hobbies include writing romantic poetry and painting graveyard scenes.

His Secret: He is in love with Tina Spicytail, Geronimo's grandfather's cook!

spin a web! **SO GET READY.**

Then she hung up.

I had to do something. My whiskers were **quivering** with fright! I did **NOT** want to see Creepella! I did **NOT** want to ride in a hearse! I did **NOT** want to go to Cacklefur Castle! I did **NOT** want to meet Creepella's family!

I quickly thought up a plan. I put on a pair of dark glasses, a hat, and a raincoat. Then I scurried to the back door. I opened it . . . and someone tripped me! I fell right on my snout.

I looked up into Creepella's green eyes.

"I know you so well, my little pumpkin," she said, smiling. "I knew you would put on a disguise and try to escape out the back!"

Creepella picked me up and shoved me into her hearse. "**Heeeeeeeeeeelp!**" I shrieked. "I'm being mousenapped!"

I was in **trouble**.

Big **trouble**.

Creepella slid into the driver's seat. "How do you like my hearse?" she asked. "Of course, it doesn't normally carry *living* mice. But I'm sure you'll be comfortable."

"**Putrid cheese puffs**, get me out of here!" I screamed.

Creepella just smiled. "You can't escape, Geronimo," she said. "You might as well get comfortable!"

"LET ME OUT!"

How could I be comfortable in a hearse? With Creepella? "Let me out!" I yelled.

Creepella winked at me. "You are going to love Cacklefur Castle, my little ghostie-whostie."

Then she began to sing a little tune.

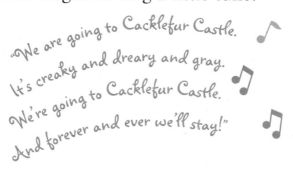

"We are going to Cacklefur Castle.
It's creaky and dreary and gray.
We're going to Cacklefur Castle.
And forever and ever we'll stay!"

I sighed and put on my seat belt. There was no escape.

Only one thought comforted me. If I ever *did* get home, I would definitely have something to *write* about!

THE VALLEY OF THE VAIN VAMPIRES

We drove all through the night. By the time dawn came, we had reached a **GLOOMY** valley. Thick trees with twisted branches grew all around.

I looked away from the trees into the valley. The mountainside was shaped like a giant skull. A creepy castle with lots of towers sat on top of it. It looked so spooky, I knew it had to be **CACKLEFUR CASTLE!**

THE VALLEY OF THE VAIN VAMPIRES

1. **Shrieking Peak**
2. **Screaming Peak**
3. **Scaredycat Mountain**
4. **Mangymouse Mountain**
5. **Cacklefur Castle**
6. **Rancidrat River**
7. **Nightmare Woods**
8. **Sleazysnot Stream**
9. **Toad Spit Brook**
10. **Putrid Pond**
11. **Ghoul's Gully**
12. **Dangerous Dale**

A muddy moat surrounded the castle. Creepella stopped the car in front of a drawbridge blocked by a gate. The gate was marked with a carved wooden sign:

CACKLEFUR CASTLE

Creepella leaned out of the car and rang a bell on the gate.

MEEEEOOOOOW!

I nearly jumped out of my fur. "What was that? I want to go **HOME**!" I squeaked.

Creepella laughed. "Calm down, my little cheesecake. It's only the *DOORBELL*!"

Someone inside the castle lowered the drawbridge. As we drove across the moat, I thought I saw two eyes gleaming from the depths of the murky water. But it must have been my imagination. Right?

A creepy castle sat on top of the skull-shaped mountain.

WELCOME TO CACKLEFUR CASTLE!

"Welcome to Cacklefur Castle!" Creepella shrieked.

She parked the car, and we walked up to the front door. I could make out a plant next to the doorway. A big plant. It had a thorny stem. It had **SPIKY** leaves. And when I looked closer, I saw the plant had white, sharp, shiny... **TEETH!**

"Rat-munching rattlesnakes!" I cried.

The plant leaned over and sniffed me. Then it bit off one of my buttons!

"Geronimo, meet Chompers, our watch plant," Creepella said.

THE VON CACKLEFUR CREST

THE CACKLEFUR WATCH PLANT

Who Is She? Her scientific name is *Horrifica dentibula*. Her nickname is Chompers. She has very sharp teeth at the end of her flower.

Her Secret: She owns a collection of toothbrushes that she guards ferociously.

I quickly turned on my cell phone. "I'm just going to call my sister," I said casually. "I want to tell her I've been mousenapped — I mean, that I'll be away for a while."

Creepella's green eyes flashed. She snatched the phone away. "No phone calls!" she snapped. "They are forbidden here!" She threw my cell phone to the plant. "Here, Chompers," she said. "A little snack for you."

The plant gulped down my phone in one mouthful! I began to lose hope. I was going to be trapped in Cacklefur Castle forever!

Creepella stepped up to the door. I followed her. I set my paw on the doormat, and it cried out, "OUCH!"

I jumped back. What kind of a place was this?

Creepella opened the door. We stepped into an enormouse hall with marble floors.

Tall windows let in the morning sunlight. Paintings of the Cacklefur family's ancestors lined the walls.

Creepella turned her snout to mine. "It's so good to be home," she said with a sigh. "How about a *kiss*, my little zombie-wombie?"

THE CACKLEFUR ANCESTORS

1. Abracadabra von Cacklefur, a medieval magician famouse for his love potions.

2. Swashbuckler von Cacklefur, a knight who fought against that mythical monster, the Three-headed Cat.

3. Cruella von Cacklefur, a charming rat. Many a rodent lost his head over Cruella. (Really—she had them all beheaded!)

1 **2** **3**

I took a step back. A cold breeze **BLEW** through the windows. The curtains whirled in the air like ghosts.

Creepella turned to the window. "This room has a lovely view of the graveyard. Isn't it romantic?"

"I want to go **HOME**!" I wailed.

Then I heard a loud cough. I turned around.

A gray rat stood there. He held a candelabra in his paw. He was tall and thin, with a *pointy* snout and whiskers that were waxed and curled.

What a curious-looking rodent!

I Can't Believe
My Ears!

"This is Boneham, our butler," Creepella said. "How are you today, Boneham?"

The thin rat bowed. "**VERY BAD**, thank you, Miss Von Cacklefur." Then he looked up and saw me. "Good heavens! We have a guest!" he said, shocked.

"This is Geronimo Stilton," Creepella declared. "We are going to be married!"

I almost fainted. "Well, that's n-n-not—" I stammered. "I mean, Creepella and I—"

"I will see you later, my little **MONSTER** pie," Creepella said. She turned to the butler. "Take care of him for me, please."

"I will do my worst, Miss Creepella," the butler said.

INSIDE CACKLEFUR CASTLE

1. Muddy moat where The Thing lives
2. Drawbridge
3. Front door
4. Chompers
5. Front hall
6. Drawing room
7. Library
8. Hall of mummies
9. Dining hall
10. Safe
11. Watchtower
12. Weapons room
13. Inner courtyard
14. Greenhouse
15. Castle grounds
16. Crocodile pool and piranha tank
17. Bedrooms
18. Guest bedroom
19. Kitchen and pantry

...the flesh-eating strawberries

...the crocodile pool

...and the piranha tank!

Boneham led me down a **very long**, **very narrow**, and **VERY DARK** hallway. He pointed out rooms in the castle as we walked.

"Over there is the greenhouse," he explained. "That is where we grow the *flesh-eating strawberries*, my pride and joy. And at the end of this hall you'll find the library, the gym, the crocodile pool, and the piranha tank."

I could not believe my ears. What kind of a house has a crocodile pool?

"And these stairs lead to the castle dungeons," Boneham continued.

BONEHAM

Who Is He? Boneham has been the Cacklefur family butler for ages. He is very devoted to the Cacklefurs and calls them "the Family." He is a snob from the tip of his tail to the tips of his curled whiskers.

His Secret: His socks stink!

My stomach rumbled. I had not eaten for hours and hours.

"Where is the kitchen?" I asked.

The butler pointed to a door. "In there. But please make sure you call it **K**itchen, with a capital **K**. Its feelings get hurt if you don't."

Then the butler coughed. "Ahem, Mr. Stilton," he began. "I have heard you are a publisher. I am working on a **MASTERPIECE**. It's entitled *The Adventures of the Cacklefur Family.* So far I have written **3 6 5** volumes. Would you mind taking a look at it?"

I gave him a card. "Give me a call when you are finished writing," I told him.

Geronimo Stilton

Publisher
THE RODENT'S GAZETTE

17 Swiss Cheese Center
New Mouse City,
Mouse Island 13131

HERE LIES THE GUEST...

Boneham stopped in front of a purple door engraved with a skull. A brass plaque on the door read **GUEST ROOM** .

Boneham opened the door and I peeked inside. It was a strange-looking room! Thick purple velvet covered the walls. It reminded me of the inside of a **pricey** coffin. Creepy!

The dresser was shiny and black. The silver handles looked like coffin handles. A large bed with four posts sat in the center of the room. Bats and spiders were carved into the posts. Over the bed hung a sign:

HERE LIES THE GUEST

How was I supposed to sleep in this chamber of horrors?

I gulped and stepped inside. How was I supposed to get any sleep in this chamber of horrors? I shivered at the thought.

Boneham cleared his throat. "We could certainly use a fire on this chilly autumn day."

I turned toward the fireplace. There was no fire.

The butler spoke again, more loudly this time. "I said, we could certainly use a fire."

Once again, I was confused. Who was Boneham talking to?

Finally, Boneham began to yell. "We need a F-I-R-E! A fire! It is cold enough to FREEZE your whiskers in here!"

Suddenly, a crackling fire began to burn in the fireplace. I stepped back, shocked. What had happened? Was this some kind of magic?

We need a fire!

Um...the mirror...

It's a real paw-puller!

"I am sorry, sir," Boneham said. "The fireplace is a bit deaf. It is more than three hundred years old, you see."

I took another step back and found myself standing next to a tall mirror. At least I thought it was a mirror. I could not see my reflection in it!

"Is something wrong with the mirror?" I asked.

"Oh, the MIRROR has probably just gone somewhere to take a nap," Boneham answered. "It's very lazy, sir. So sorry."

A deaf fireplace? A lazy

mirror? What kind of a place was this?

Boneham walked toward the door. "One more thing, sir," he said. "Be careful of the *carpet*. It's a real paw-puller. And if you need anything, just **YELL**."

The butler left and closed the door. I looked down at the carpet, curious. Without warning, it pulled out from under me. **SPLAT!** I fell flat on my snout. Then the carpet rolled up—with me inside it!

Boneham opened the door. "I told you, sir. The *carpet* is a real paw-puller!" Then he shut the door behind him.

I could not take it anymore. I was hungry. I was tired. And now I was rolled up in a paw-pulling carpet!

"*I want to go home!*" I wailed.

EARTHWORM LIVER
AND LEECH LARD

I unrolled myself from the carpet. There was no way I could sleep in this awful room. I decided to search for something to eat instead. I was so hungry, I would have given my left paw for a cheese sandwich!

As I walked down the hallway, a delicious smell wafted toward me. My whiskers twitched.

Sniff . . . Sniff . . . It smelled like stew!

I followed my snout until I found the kitchen. It was an enormouse room with a brick ceiling and stone floor.

I saw a rat stirring a pot over the stove. If I were being polite, I might describe him as a **HEAVY** rat with a stained apron and waxed

CHEF STEWRAT

Who Is He? The Cacklefur family cook. He loves the opera. He is always trailed by a cloud of gnats. That's probably because he hasn't washed since Christmas—exactly which Christmas, nobody knows!

His Secret: He dreams of selling his stew around the world. And he is in love with Madame Latomb!

whiskers. But I was tired and hungry, and not feeling very polite. And so I'll tell you that he was a very fat sewer rat with a filthy, smelly apron and greasy whiskers. Not at all the kind of rat a mouse of refined taste likes to see in a kitchen!

The cook was *humming* a tune while he stirred the pot:

" Open your snout.
Come and pig out!
My stew is a treat.
The best thing you'll eat!
Eat and eat until
you're fat.
And you will be a
happy rat!"

The cook saw me and beckoned me closer. Now I could see a cloud of tiny **bugs** flying around his head.

He held out a spoon. "Do me a favor and taste this," he said.

I was so hungry, I slurped the stew right from the spoon.

"Very good," I said, licking my whiskers. "In fact, it's excellent!"

The cook grinned. "**Nobody makes stew like mine**. It's the best around!"

He grabbed a bowl and filled it to the brim for me. I grabbed it eagerly. *Maybe this trip wasn't so bad after all,* I thought. The

Chef Stewrat's great-great-great-great-great grandfather!

delicious stew made up for all of the horrible things I had found so far.

"The stew is quite wonderful," I said. "Would you mind telling me what's in it?"

"Of course not," the cook said, beaming. "Let's see. There is earthworm liver . . . leech lard . . . black scorpion claws . . . wasp stingers . . . bat thighs . . . crushed red termites . . . shark fins . . . piranha teeth . . . iguana claws . . . viper venom . . . snake spleen . . . plus a little salt and pepper!"

My stomach lurched. "**WHAT**?"

The cook smiled. He grabbed a cockroach crawling across the stove. Then he tossed it into the stew.

"How do you think my stew got so good?"

he asked. "It is because I keep adding surprise ingredients!"

I watched in horror as he took off one of his SMELLY socks and threw it into the stew. "Just a little bit of flavor," he said. "Don't want to overdo it." He pulled out the sock. "I will tell you a secret," he whispered. "This stew has been simmering in this pot for the last five hundred years! I inherited it from my great-great-great-great-great grandfather!"

I felt betrayed. I felt sick. I felt dizzy.

"I want to go HOME!" I wailed.

Just then, a loud female voice rang through the kitchen. "Chef Stewrat!"

The cook turned around. His eyes gleamed with excitement. "Madame Latomb!" he cried.

SING FOR ME, MY LITTLE WERE-CANARY!

A very strange mouse entered the kitchen. She wore an old-fashioned dress trimmed with lace. A BAT-SHAPED necklace hung around her neck. She had a huge pile of white hair on top of her head. When she got closer, I noticed she had a strange **odor** — like dead flowers.

But that was not the only strange thing about Madame Latomb. I swore I heard a growl when she came in. *Grrrrrrrrrr*. But I could not tell where the sound was coming from!

Madame Latomb smiled at the cook.

"Chef Stewrat, I need today's menu," she said.

MADAME LATOMB

Who Is She? The housekeeper of the Cacklefur family. She plays the violin and collects dolls. Her hairstyle hides her ferocious were-canary. It's like a werewolf, but it's a canary—and a lot scarier when the moon is full!

Her Secret: She is in love with Professor Frankenstein!

"Of course, Madame Latomb," said the cook in a sweet voice. "You do look lovely today. Here is the menu."

GRILLED STEW WITH TOADSTOOLS

STEW PIE WITH FRIED STEW STICKS

SCRAMBLED STEW WITH STEW SAUCE

STEW ICE CREAM

"Thank you, Chef," Madame Latomb said. She turned and left the kitchen. And as she walked away, she sang a strange little song.

"Sing for me, my dearie.
Sing for me, my little were-canary!"

As she sang, I saw a little yellow bird pop out of Madame Latomb's hair! The bird looked at me and growled.

I shivered. I didn't know what a WERE-CANARY was. But I was sure it wasn't nice!

YOU'RE LOOKING SO
PALE, SHIVEREEN!

I left the kitchen, rubbing my grumbling belly. Somehow, I had to find a way out of Cacklefur Castle. I opened the first door I could find and stepped inside.

I found myself in an enormouse hall filled with strange-looking rodents. I looked down at my paws. The marble floor was lizard green. I looked up. Candlelight cast ghostly shadows on the walls.

I felt a paw on my shoulder and *squeaked* in surprise. It was **CREEPELLA**!

"Hello, my little zombie-wombie," she said, stroking my whiskers. "How do you like the castle?"

"I want to go HOME!" I cried.

Creepella ignored me. She grabbed my paw and dragged me into the hall.

"I'm going to introduce you to the family, Geronimo," she said. "Please don't embarrass me."

Before I could reply, a teenage mouse ran up to us. She looked like a smaller version of Creepella. She had the same shiny gray fur, and she seemed very fond of the color purple. She wore a purple shirt and jeans. She carried a bat-shaped purse. And perched on top of her shoulder was a real live **chameleon**!

"Hello, **Auntie**," the little mouse said. "How nice to see you!"

Creepella hugged her. "**Shivereen**, you look pale! How lovely!"

"Thanks," answered Shivereen. "I love your dress. It's so... **mysterious**."

SHIVEREEN

Who Is She? She is Creepella's favorite niece. She copies Creepella in every way. She has a pet chameleon named Moldy. She dreams of working in the world of fashion.

Her Secret: She keeps a diary hidden under her mattress.

Creepella pushed me forward. "Shivereen, I'd like you meet Geronimo Stilton. We are going to be *married*!"

"That's not exactly—" I began. But Shivereen interrupted me.

"When is the **wedding**?" she squeaked.

"**NEVER**!" I screamed. Enough was enough!

"Don't listen to Geronimo," Creepella said, taking her niece's arm. "He's just a little tired from our trip. Now tell me, do you have a mousefriend yet?"

The two mice walked away, chattering. I looked around the hall, hoping to find a friendly face—or a way to escape.

I saw something that might help. An **old-fashioned** phone hung on the wall. I crept over to it, as quiet as a mouse, and quickly dialed my sister, Thea.

"Hello, Thea," I whispered. "It's me, Geronimo. I've been mousenapp——"

Suddenly, the telephone began to scream! "Put down the phone, cheddarface! No phone calls allowed! No phone calls allowed!"

Creepella ran over and hung up the phone. "Well done, Telephone," she told the phone. "Geronimo was being very naughty. Very naughty indeed."

"I want to go **HOME**!" I wailed.

The mice in the hall all looked at me.

"That Geronimo Stilton is a strange mouse," they whispered.

PUT DOWN N THE PHONE, CHEDDARFACE!

SNIP AND SNAP, THE SPOOKY TWINS

Boneham walked into the hall, carrying a gong. He put earplugs in his ears. Then he struck the gong with a mallet. The loud sound rang through the hall.

Gooooooooooooooooooong!

I held my ears and followed everyone into the dining hall. Chef Stewrat was wheeling in a tray with the stew pot.

"Stew is ready!" he cried. "**Come and get it!**"

My stomach lurched at the thought of more stew. As everyone scrambled for a seat at the long dining table, I saw my chance. I quickly ducked under the table.

Unfortunately, I wasn't alone. I found

SNIP AND SNAP

Who Are They? These twins are very smart and very good with computers. They are exactly alike, perfectly mean, and truly annoying!

Their Secret: They own a collection of tricks that they use to scare guests staying at Cacklefur Castle!

myself staring at two young mice who looked exactly alike! At first, they did not look like the other Cacklefurs. They both had very neat hair and very normal-looking clothes. But they each had a wicked gleam in their eyes.

I suddenly heard Creepella shout, "I just looked out the window. Who painted flowers on my hearse? If I catch him, I'll tear his whiskers out one by one!"

"It must have been Snip and Snap!" said Madame Latomb.

Beside me, the twin mice began to giggle.

KAFKA, THE FAITHFUL COCKROACH

Before I could question the boys, I felt something lick my ankle! Then I heard a bark. "**ARF!**"

"Kafka has sniffed out something!" shrieked Creepella.

I turned around and looked at my ankle. A huge cockroach sat there! It was sitting on its hind legs and barking like a dog. "**ARF! ARF! ARF!**"

"Quiet!" I hissed.

But it was too late. Madame Latomb lifted the tablecloth. "*Come on out, you little scoundrels!*" she commanded.

Snip and Snap crawled out from under the

table. I had no choice but to follow them.

Creepella shrieked. "My hearse used to be so gloomy! And now it looks cheerful!"

"*HE DID IT!*" said Snip, pointing to Snap.

"*HE DID IT!*" said Snap, pointing to Snip.

The boys looked at each other. Then they pointed at me! "No, he did it!" they squeaked.

"I did not!" I protested.

Creepella batted her green eyes. "Naughty boy, Geronimo. You must give me a *kiss*, and I'll forgive you."

Before I could protest, she puckered up her snout and kissed me!

ARF ARF ARF

KAFKA THE COCKROACH

KAFKA'S HOUSE

KAFKA

Who Is He? The much-loved pet cockroach of the Cacklefur family. His cockroach house is in the courtyard, but he loves to sleep in Shivereen's bed. She takes him for a walk every morning.

His Secret: He can't get enough Cockroach Crunchies!

THE JOKING GHOST

Everyone sat down at the table. But the moment my bottom touched the seat, there was a loud, embarrassing noise.

Pffffffffffft!

"Excuse me," I said, turning bright red. "I didn't mean—"

Then I realized what had happened. Someone had put a whoopee cushion on my chair! "Who put this here?" I shrieked.

"It wasn't US this time!" said Snip and Snap.

I didn't believe them. But they were telling the truth.

"It was **Booey**, sir," explained Boneham. "He is the *castle ghost*. He loves to play jokes. He's very playful."

BOOEY THE POLTERGEIST

Who Is He? The ghost of Cacklefur Castle. This young ghost is a poltergeist, which means he likes to play tricks on everyone.

His Secret: He is afraid of scary movies—but he watches them anyway!

Just then, my water glass floated off the table. Then the water poured onto my lap!

"Booey seems to like you a lot, sir," said the butler.

I **SHUDDERED**. What would Booey do if he *didn't* like me?

Everyone began to eat their stew. I looked into my bowl and frowned. Inside the bubbling goo, I saw one of my own buttons! I saw a yellow canary feather, too. I pushed away the bowl in DISGUST.

"Excuse me, Chef," I asked. "May I have something else to eat? A salad, maybe?"

Chef Stewrat looked *angry*. "Are you saying you don't like my stew?"

Everyone at the table stared at me.

"That Geronimo Stilton is a strange mouse," they murmured.

The chef sighed. "I can make you a salad if you want. How about some poison ivy with slime dressing? Or sewer algae with moldy mushrooms and some nice pond scum on top?"

That Geronimo Stilton is one strange mouse!

I turned as pale as a piece of mozzarella. "Um, how about some fruit instead?"

"I have just the thing," Chef Stewrat said. "How about a bowl of FLESH-EATING strawberries? Their teeth are nice and sharp."

I turned even PALER. "No, thank you," I said weakly.

"Well, what will it be?" asked the chef. "Some snake steak? Or some nice toxic tiger fish? It's fresh from the moat."

"I think I'll just skip supper," I said. My poor stomach growled.

"Have some toadstool tea, my little bat wing," said Creepella. "It will make your tummy feel better!"

THE THING HAS A TUMMY ACHE!

I turned down the toadstool tea and left. I was walking down the hallway when, suddenly, the castle walls began to **shake**! Then I heard a strange rumbling sound.

BUURRRRRPPPP!!

My fur stood on end. "Putrid cheese puffs!" I cried. "It's an earthquake!"

Boneham the butler walked up to me. "It is not an earthquake, sir. It is The Thing."

Boneham led me to the window. He pointed to the green, slimy moat that surrounded the castle. "The Thing has a tummy ACHE," he explained.

"What thing?" I squeaked. I **leaned** out the window for a better look. The moat

THE THING

What Is It? Nobody knows. If they did, it wouldn't be called The Thing! Nobody has ever seen it, but everyone knows it is enormouse. It lives in the moat and eats whatever crosses its path.

Its Secret: The Thing is very shy. That is why nobody has ever seen it!

GURGLED and BUBBLED below.

Boneham pulled me back. "Be careful, sir. The Thing will eat anything it can. Don't get too close to the moat. We've lost many guests that way."

"Th-thank you, Boneham," I stammered.

I scurried back to my room. My mind was racing faster than a HAMSTER ON A WHEEL. Cacklefur Castle was too much for me. The mouse-eating Thing in the moat was the last straw. There had to be some way to escape! I looked out the window. I am afraid of heights. But I was not *too* far from the ground. Maybe, just maybe, I could . . .

I put my plan into action. I took the sheets off the bed. I tied them together to make one long rope. I tied one end of the rope to the bedpost. Then I dropped the rest out the window.

I took a deep breath and began to climb down.

Suddenly, the sheets began to **swing back and forth**! Above me, the window shutters began to rattle.

Then the window—yes, the window—began to tease me!

"NYAH NYAH NYAH NYAH NYAH!" the window sang.

I gripped the sheets tightly. I did not want to fall!

"**I want to go HOME**!" I screamed.

Below me, I saw Boneham driving up in a strange car. There was a big net attached to it.

"Hold on, sir!" he called up.

The sheets twisted once

more. I lost my grip. I fell... **Plop!**

...and I landed safely in Boneham's net.

The net dropped me on the grass. Kafka the cockroach ran up. He lifted his leg—and peed on my pants!

"Why is this happening to me?" I sobbed. "I am a good mouse. I don't deserve this!"

I ran back up to my room and jumped in bed. I pulled the covers over my head. Maybe this was all just a bad dream!

But it wasn't. The mattress began to **TICKLE** my tail!

Hold on, sir!
Hold on, sir!
Hold on, sir!

I jumped out of bed. I decided to take a hot bath instead, to calm my nerves. I turned on the water. Then I jumped back.

The water was STEAMING HOT! I tried another knob. This time, the water was **freezing**! Actual ice cubes floated on the water!

The bathtub laughed at me. "**Ha-ha-ha!**"

I gave up on the bath. But there was one thing I really *had* to do....

I slowly walked up to the **toilet**. I had to go, but I was a little nervous. What would the toilet be like? It looked scary. It was black with skulls and crossbones on the tank.

Slowly, I lifted the lid. The toilet began to gurgle.

"Use me if you dare.
You're in for quite a scare!
Maybe I'll flood the room.
Or suck you to your doom!"

My whiskers quivered in fear. I backed away slowly.

The toilet kept singing. The window shutters kept clapping. The bed kept laughing. Then the closet joined in. It began opening and shutting it s door.

BANG! BANG! BANG! BANG! BANG! BANG!

I covered my ears and ran out of the **GUEST ROOM**.

"I want to go HOOOOME!" I wailed.

gurgle!

THE ATTACK OF THE FLESH-EATING STRAWBERRIES

I bumped into the twins in the hall. "Where is the bathroom?" I asked them.

Snip and Snap pointed to a nearby door. "It's in there!"

"Thank you!" I said. How polite.

But when I opened the door, I saw I wasn't in a bathroom. I was in a greenhouse. Clay pots with small green plants filled the room.

For a moment, I thought I heard a noise. Munch! Munch! Munch!

I moved closer to the plants. They looked so pretty! Each plant was loaded with red, sweet-smelling fruit.

"Strawberries!" I said. "At last, something

normal to eat!" I reached out with my paw to pick a strawberry...and **it bit me**!

"Ow!" I cried. I looked down. The little strawberry had a mouth and tiny teeth!

"I want to go **HOME**!" I wailed.

All at once, the strawberries jumped out of their pots. They began to chase me!

Munch! Munch! Munch! Their little teeth chomped as they got closer and closer....

Luckily, at that moment Boneham ran in. He was carrying a can of sardines. "Dinnertime, my sweets!" he called out.

The strawberries ran to Boneham. He fed them the sardines. They gobbled them up like a pack of cats at a mouse buffet.

I sighed with relief and headed for the door. It was then that I noticed a sign on the wall.

FLESH-EATING STRAWBERRIES
ENTER AT YOUR OWN RISK.
(BUT YOU DON'T REALLY WANT TO ENTER, DO YOU?)

I ran from the flesh-eating strawberries.

Then I heard a giggle. I turned to see Snip and Snap.

"YOU ROTTEN LITTLE RATLETS!" I cried. The twins just laughed and ran away.

I scurried down the hall, looking for a bathroom door. In the dim light, I saw a small yellow figure flying toward me.

It was Madame Latomb's were-canary!

The little bird chomped on my finger with its sharp beak.

"Ow!" I squeaked.

Madame Latomb stepped out of a door.

"Come here, my little songbird," she said.

The were-canary flew to Madame Latomb and disappeared inside her huge hairdo. I wanted to tell her what I thought of her little terror, but I really, really had to find a bathroom now.

I looked at the nearest door. It had a sign with teeny-weeny print on it.

> DO NOT OPEN THIS DOOR!
> DON'T EVEN THINK ABOUT IT!
> REALLY! DON'T TRY IT!

Boneham ran up to me. "Please don't open this door, sir," he said. "We have lost many guests this way."

"But what is inside?" I asked.

Boneham's *whiskers* twitched. "I do not know, sir," he said. "But I am sure it is not very nice!"

A SURPRISE IN THE DARK

I had had enough surprises for one day. I found another door. This one did not have any signs on it. I opened it.

I stepped into a dark room. I felt on the wall for a light switch, but there was none.

Then I made out a shape in the dark. A toilet!

Relieved, I sat down and began to take care of business. When I was done, I reached out to grab the toilet paper. I touched something that felt like toilet paper. So I gave it a pull.

I flushed the toilet. Then I remembered I had a small flashlight in my pocket. I took it out, turned it on...

...and found myself face-to-face with a
ᴍᴜᴍᴍᴛ!

"ʜₑₑₑₑₑₗₚ!" I shrieked. With horror,
I realized I hadn't found toilet paper at
all. I had found the wrappings of a mouse
mummy!

My paws trembled. I dropped the flashlight.
The light went out.

"Heeeeeelp!" I screamed again.

The door opened. Creepella stepped
inside.

"There you are, my little ghostie-whostie," she said. "What are you doing in the staff bathroom? This is where my grandfather kept his mummies. He was fixing them. You didn't hurt them, did you?"

I was still in shock. "M-M-M-MUMMIES!" I stammered.

Suddenly, I felt someone step on my tail. I whirled around.

Snip and Snap stood there, giggling.

"*HE DID IT!*" said Snip.

"*HE DID IT!*" said Snap.

"I want to go HOME!" I wailed.

The Cacklefur family gathered in the hallway. They shook their heads.

"That Geronimo Stilton is a strange mouse!" they cried.

I WANT TO
GO HOME!

Still shaking, I made my way back to the guest room. At least there were no mummies there. But I got lost in the **LONG HALLWAYS**.

As I searched for my door, I noticed something on the floor. I reached down and picked it up. It was an **old** piece of paper. I raised it to my snout. It was a treasure map!

TREASURE MAP

Take three steps to the right. Take two steps to the left. Take one more step to the right. Then place your paw on the stone marked with the letter T.

Even though I was tired, and scared, and hungry, I had to follow the map. I was too *curious* to resist.

I took three steps

to the right. Then two steps to the left. Then one more step to the right. I found myself facing a big stone in the wall with the letter **T** carved in it. **T** for treasure? Excited, I pushed on the stone…

…and fell down a tunnel!

I tumbled down…down…down.

Finally, I found myself in a **cold**, **dark** room. I stood up and brushed the dust off my fur. I looked around.

Cobwebs dangled from the corners. A grinning skeleton hung from the wall.

I took a step back…and fell right into a coffin!

I jumped out . . . and bumped into a suit of armor!

I fell back...and tripped over a tombstone!

I stood up...and found myself holding a mummy!

Then I heard a ghostly wail.

"Booooooooooooooooooo!"

"I want to go HOME!" I screamed.

Suddenly, all the lights came on.

In the light, I could see that everything was fake!

The dust was made of flour. The cobwebs were made of cotton candy. The skeleton was made of plastic. The coffin was made of rubber. The suit of armor was made of soda cans. The tombstone was made of cardboard. The mummy was made of toilet paper. And the ghostly sound was coming from a speaker on the wall.

I also saw a sign on the wall:

SNIP AND SNAP'S
COLLECTION OF TRICKS
PAWS OFF!
(THAT MEANS YOU!)

I should have known. Those twin terrors were behind this!

I was fed up. I found a staircase and ran up the steps.

Snip and Snap were in the hall, smiling.

"I know you left that treasure map for me to find," I growled.

"*HE DID IT!*" said Snip.

"*HE DID IT!*" said Snap.

Boneham shook his head. "Snip and Snap have struck again, sir!"

PROFESSOR FRANKENSTEIN'S WILL

I was looking for my room again when I noticed that all of the Cacklefurs had left the dining room table. They were gathered in front of the fireplace.

Suddenly, I remembered why Creepella had brought me here in the first place. For the reading of her grandfather's **WILL**!

They say that curiosity kills the **CAT**. But I am a mouse, after all, and a very curious one at that. I stood in the background and listened to what the family was saying.

"Poor Professor Frankenstein," said one mouse. "Remember how much he loved mummy jokes?"

"Yes, he told many mummy $jokes$," said

another. "Many, many mummy jokes."

"Maybe *too* many mummy jokes!"

The chattering stopped when a plump rodent walked in.

"It's BYRON BADNEWS, the family lawyer," the Cacklefurs whispered.

Byron Badnews was an unpleasant-looking mouse. He carried a small silver box shaped like a coffin.

The lawyer cleared his throat. "Attention, Cacklefurs!" he announced. "The moment you have been waiting for is here!"

Byron tapped the lid of the coffin. "In this box I have"—he paused dramatically—

BYRON BADNEWS

"Professor Frankenstein's **WILL**!"

The family began to **chatter** in excitement.

"What would you do if he left you the castle?" asked one mouse.

"I would turn it into a HORROR museum," replied another mouse.

"I would turn it into an **amousement** park," said another.

"I would open a *vacation* lodge," said another.

Chef Stewrat tapped his paw impatiently on the floor. "**CHEESE CHUNKS!**" he cried. "Are you going to read the will or what? I have to go stir my stew."

Byron Badnews sniffed. "You seem to have your tail in a twitch," he said. "Very well. I will read the will. Cacklefur Castle goes to..."

Byron Badnews lifted the lid of the coffin.

A stream of black ink **SHOT** out and squirted him in the snout!

"Who did this?" he bellowed.

"**HE DID IT!**" said Snip.

"**HE DID IT!**" said Snap.

Suddenly, a bolt of lightning struck the castle.

Thunder shook the castle walls.

BOOOOOOOOM!

All the candles blew out. The room was as dark as the inside of a tomcat's tummy.

An icy wind swirled through the room. It froze the tips of my whiskers.

"Isn't this fun?" Creepella asked, grabbing my paw. "I told you you'd have a good time at Cacklefur Castle."

A good time? This was the worst time I'd ever had in my life! "I want to go **HOME**!" I wailed.

At that moment, the doors to the dining hall flew open. A shadowy figure stood in the doorway.

"It's Grandfather's GHOST!" the Cacklefurs all cried at once.

"I'm not a ghost," said the figure. "I am alive and squeaking, my dear family!"

The lights came back on. A small, skinny mouse stood in the doorway. His face was the color of moldy cheese. The white fur on his head struck straight up. He wore a stained white lab coat. He walked with a limp and leaned on a cane.

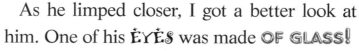

As he limped closer, I got a better look at him. One of his EYES was made OF GLASS!

Professor Frankenstein adjusted his false teeth. Then he gazed at his family.

"What a nice family reunion," he said. "Why does everyone look so sad? You look

PROFESSOR FRANKENSTEIN

Who Is He? A scientist who studies ancient Egypt. He is an expert on mummies and tombs. He is a little clumsy and has had many accidents in his lab. So far, he has lost an eye, an ear, a little finger, and a toe.

His Secret: He dreams of being a stand-up comic.

like you're at a **FUNERAL**. Ha!"

"Grandfather! You're alive!" shouted the Cacklefurs.

"Of course I am," Professor Frankenstein cackled. "I was picking mushrooms in Nightmare Wood. I fell asleep under the Tree of Eternal Rest. If a bat had not peed on my snout, I would never have woken up."

The mice all nodded their heads in surprise.

The professor waved his cane in the air. "Sorry to disappoint you, family!" he squeaked. "Cacklefur Castle is mine! So paws off—or you'll be sorry!"

Everyone in the dining hall looked slightly afraid.

Professor Frankenstein smiled. "Don't look so glum. I have some BLOODCURDLING jokes to tell you. You will laugh your heads off!"

PROFESSOR FRANKENSTEIN'S BLOODCURDLING JOKES

 What is Count Dracula's favorite dog?
A bloodhound!

Where do ghosts go on vacation?
To the Dead Sea!

 Why was the skeleton afraid of the dark?
Because it didn't have any guts!

What kind of music does a mummy like best?
Wrap music!

Why do ghosts make good cheerleaders?
Because they have a lot of spirit!

 A skeleton went to see the doctor. The doctor opened the door. He looked at the skeleton and said, "Aren't you a little late?"

SPEAKING OF MUMMIES...

The professor slapped me on the shoulder.

"Did you like my jokes?" he asked. "And who are you, anyway?"

"The name is Stilton, *Geronimo Stilton*," I said.

Creepella walked up and *kissed* me on the snout. "Isn't he sweet?" she asked. "He and I are getting married."

I cleared my throat. "Actually, we are not—"

But Professor Frankenstein interrupted me. "So this is your latest **VICTIM**—I mean fiancé," he said. "What is your name again? Gabriel?"

"Geronimo!" I said.

He pinched my cheek. "So when will the wedding be, Gideon?"

"**NEVER!**" I said firmly.

He ignored me. "Well, then, Gerald, you had better treat my little Creepella well. If anyone dares to treat my granddaughter badly, I will turn him into a 𝕄𝕌𝕄𝕄𝕐!" He waved his cane.

The Cacklefurs all agreed. "That's right! We pity the mouse who mistreats our Creepella!"

I was quaking in my fur. "Of course, Professor," I said. "I will treat Creepella well. *Rodent's word of honor!*"

Professor Frankenstein pulled a watch from his pocket. "I must go, my dear Gary," he said. "The mummy of the great Tutankhamouse has arrived. I must get to work!"

Before the professor left, he told another joke. "Why did the werewolf cross the road? To eat the chicken on the other side. HA!"

With that, he limped down the hallway, still laughing.

Chef Stewrat came up to me. "I should get started on your wedding cake. Stew cake with stew frosting, of course. When will the wedding be?"

"NEVER!" I yelled at the top of my voice.

The Cacklefurs all stared at me. "That Geronimo Stilton is a strange mouse!" they whispered.

WAH! WAH! WAH!

The doorbell meowed.

MEEEEOOOOOOOOOW!

Boneham scurried to lift the drawbridge. "It must be Mr. Von Cacklefur!" he said.

A few minutes later, a **VERY THIN** rat came through the door. He was dressed in black and wore a top hat. I had met him before. It was Boris von Cacklefur, Creepella's father!

He held out a paw to me. "Hello there, Geronimo," he said. "You look well. Too bad. We're having a sale on coffins this week. HA~HA!"

"Nice to see you, Mr. Von Cacklefur," I said.

Then another sound rang through the hall.

Wah! Wah! Wah!

Curious, we all ran to the window.

Boneham took a pair of binoculars out of his pocket. He looked down.

"Cheddar biscuits!" he exclaimed. "What is that?"

I looked through the binoculars. There was a small basket in front of the drawbridge. And it sounded as if the basket was...crying.

We all ran outside.

Inside the basket was a tiny bundle

wrapped in a blanket. The butler moved aside the blanket to reveal a baby mouse!

"**MOLDY MUMMIES!**" cried Professor Frankenstein.

"A little orphan," said Boneham.

"He's so small," said Boris.

"He's so sweet!" said Creepella.

"My, he can cry," said Madame Latomb.

Snip said, "He must be..."

"...hungry!" Snap said.

Chef Stewrat clapped his paws together. "He needs some stew!"

The members of the Cacklefur family surrounded the baby. The little mouselet stopped crying. He opened his eyes and looked at them all. Then he smiled.

All of the Cacklefurs smiled back.

THE SECRET OF THE CACKLEFUR FAMILY

"We must have a **BIG FAMILY MEETING**!" shouted Professor Frankenstein.

The entire family gathered in the library.

"Ladies and gentlemice, rodents and rats, dead and alive, family and friends," began the professor. "Even you, Garrett. We must make an important decision. We have found a little baby. What should we do?"

Boris von Cacklefur placed his paw on his heart. "I hate to be a *mushy* mouse. But this makes me think of a poem by Emily Dickinson:

"That *Love* is all there is,
is all we know of *Love*."

I felt my eyes fill with tears. What a lovely poem!

Boris went on. "We all know the Cacklefur family secret," he said. "We love one another. With love, we can do anything!"

The mice nodded in agreement.

"This little mouselet needs our love," said Boris. "And we have plenty to give him."

Creepella stood up. "Let's vote on it. If you think we should adopt the orphan mouse, raise your paw!"

Every Cacklefur raised a paw.

"This mouselet is no longer an orphan," said Boris. "As of today, he is a **CACKLEFUR**!"

The Cacklefurs all cheered.

I took the baby in my paws. "What a sweet little snout he has!" I said. "What will you call him? He needs a name."

Creepella passed around a piece of paper. "Everyone write down a name," she said. When the Cacklefurs were done, she read the names out loud.

MUMMYKINS?   FROGGY?

HOWLER?   SKUNKY?

ZIGZAG?

SKELETINO?   CREEPERS?

SKULLY?

BATRICK?   SPIDERRAT?

TOADIE?

STEWIE?   SCREAMER?   IGOR?

MUSHMOUSE?

FESTER?   GRIMY?

SPOOKSTER?

SPECTER?   SLIMER?

DREARY?

"Um, don't you think those names are a bit weird for a baby?" I asked.

"That's it!" the Cacklefurs shouted. "We'll call him Baby!"

Just then, I felt something wet and warm on my jacket.

"Um, I think the little Cacklefur has done a wee-wee!" I said.

OUR LOVE IS STRONGER THAN CHEESE

Chef Stewrat ran to the kitchen. "I must get him a bottle of stew! It is just what he needs."

I put Baby in a COFFIN-SHAPED CRADLE. Madame Latomb took out her violin and played him a lullaby:

Go to sleep, little Cacklefur.

GO TO SLEEP, LITTLE
CACKLEFUR,
YOUR FAMILY IS NEAR.
WE WILL ALL WATCH OVER YOU,
TO US YOU ARE DEAR.
SO GO TO SLEEP.
GO TO SLEEP, IF YOU PLEASE.
OUR LOVE FOR YOU
IS STRONGER THAN CHEESE!

STEW POWER!

I *kissed* Baby. Then I decided to walk around the castle. Somehow, the Cacklefurs did not seem so scary anymore.

Because I love books, I went to the library. Old rare books filled the shelves. I flipped through the pages. Some of the books were so old they were written by monks! What treasures!

Before printing was invented, monks wrote books by hand. They illustrated them with wonderful paintings.

Then I found a large book on a tall wooden stand. The leather cover was the color of American cheese. The book looked quite old.

The title caught my eye: *The History of Cacklefur Castle.*

I sat in a comfortable chair next to the fireplace. Then I began to read.

"**Cacklefur Castle is built on a skull-shaped hill . . .**"

A blast of thunder interrupted my reading. **Bam!**

The window flew open. A huge oak tree crashed into the room. Its branches were flaming. It must have been struck by lightning!

The curtains caught fire. Soon the flames would race toward the bookshelves. All of those beautiful rare books!

I ran out of the room. "The library is on

fire!" I **SCREAMED**.

I looked for something to put out the fire with. I pushed open a door and found myself in the kitchen. The cart of stew was right in front of me. . . .

I had an id**ea**. I pushed the cart down the hall as fast as I could. When I got to the library, I dumped the stew pot onto the flames!

The fire went out, as if by magic. I fell to the floor, exhausted.

By now, all of the Cacklefur family had arrived in the library.

The stew put out the fire as if by magic.

"What is it?" asked the professor.

"What happened?" asked Boneham.

"The library…" Snip began.

"…was on fire!" Snap finished.

"Geronimo put out the **FIRE**!" Shivereen said.

"Geronimo is a hero!" announced Madame Latomb.

Creepella beamed. "Good for you, my little bat wing!"

Chef Stewrat smiled. "That is what I call Stew Power!"

The Cacklefurs gathered around me. Professor Frankenstein slapped me on the shoulder.

"You saved the library," he said. "**YOU ARE ONE OF THE FAMILY NOW**, George."

I sighed. "*My name is Geronimo!*"

GOOD-BYE, DEAR CACKLEFURS

The sun was sinking in the sky. Yes, all of these amazing adventures happened in just one day!

"Get ready, my little **CHEDDAR PUFF**," Creepella said to me. "We're going back to New Mouse City."

Creepella took my arm and led me to the dining hall.

"But we just got here!" I protested. Believe it or not, I was starting to enjoy myself.

Suddenly, the lights went out. I expected to hear a blast of thunder again.

Instead, I heard a cheer. "Hooray for Geronimo Stilton!"

When the lights came back on, the whole Cacklefur family was standing there. They had hung a banner in the hall:

COME BACK SOON, GERONIMO...DEAD OR ALIVE!

Shivereen went to the piano. She played **"THE WAILING WALTZ."** Madame Latomb played along on her violin.

Creepella grabbed me by the tail.

"This **DANCE** is for me, my little spiderweb!"

We waltzed around the hall. Candles cast a soft glow of light in the room.

"This is my favorite waltz," Creepella said. "And you are my favorite mouse. When are we going to get married?"

I remembered Professor Frankenstein's warning and turned pale. "Well, er, I—"

Luckily, the professor stood up to make an announcement.

"Quiet, everyone!" he shouted. Then he walked over and hugged me.

"It's a shame you have to leave, dear Gerbil," he said. "But before you go, we would like to give you something to say thank you."

Professor Frankenstein gave me a black plaque. There was gold writing on it:

THIS PLAQUE IS DEDICATED
TO OUR NEW FRIEND

GERONIMO STILTON
HE BRAVELY SAVED THE
CACKLEFUR FAMILY LIBRARY

Boris gathered everyone together. "Time for a picture!" he shouted. "Say cheese!"

I put on my best smile. But then I felt someone pinch my tail. I turned around.

Too late! The camera snapped the picture.

"How nice," said Boneham. "Now you will **always** be a part of the **Cacklefur family**."

I looked at the picture. "At least my back will be," I said.

Creepella took my arm. "Ready, my little pumpkin? It's time to go."

All of the Cacklefurs looked very sad.

Snip and Snap gave me a small present. "It's for you, Geronimo!" they said.

I was moved. Maybe they weren't such

BAD little mice after all.

"Thank you," I said.

I opened the present. It was a small coffin. "How nice," I said. I opened the lid. A small rubber skeleton popped out — and punched me in the snout!

"Whose idea was this?" I asked angrily.

"*HE DID IT!*" said Snip.

"*HE DID IT!*" said Snap.

Shivereen brushed away a tear. "Can I call you Uncle Geronimo?" she asked. "I can't wait for the *wedding*. When will it be?"

"**NEVER!**" I shrieked.

Professor Frankenstein looked at his watch. "It's getting late, Godfrey. You really should be going. We will miss you, Gilroy!"

"The name is Geronimo," I corrected him.

I knew it was time to go. But I did not want to leave without giving a speech.

"My dear rodent friends," I began. "I just met you. But I feel like I have known you all my life. You will always be—"

I couldn't finish the sentence. Creepella drove the hearse right into the dining hall! She grabbed my arm and pulled me inside.

"Time to go to New Mouse City, my little spiderkins!"

We **SPED** off. Behind me, I heard the Cacklefurs cheer, "Hurrah for Geronimo Stilton. He is a strange mouse—but he is a **true friend**!"

AS RARE AS FINE CHEDDAR...

We drove away from the Valley of the Vain Vampires. I realized I finally had an idea for a book! I would call it **THE SECRET OF CACKLEFUR CASTLE**.

The Cacklefurs were definitely weird. We were so different! Yet they were very close to my heart.

I learned something **IMPORTANT** at Cacklefur Castle. There are many mice who are different from us. But you can't judge a mouse by his or her fur. You must look into his or her heart! If you are lucky, you may find a friend there.

True friendship is as rare as fine cheddar. It is a real gift. It is wonderful to discover that the world is full of friends we don't know yet. That is the truth...or my name is not *Geronimo Stilton*!

Geronimo's Joke Contest Winners!

Special thanks to all my mouse friends who sent me jokes! All the jokes were absolutely hilari-mouse. In fact, I laughed so hard, I almost broke my funny bone! Here are some of my favorites.

If a mouse lost his tail, where would he go to get a new one?
A re-tail store!
From Flannery in Washington State

When should a mouse carry an umbrella?
When it's raining cats and dogs!
From Caleb in Maryland

What animal is a tattletale?
A pig. It always squeals on you!
From Emily in Ohio

What's a mouse's favorite state?
Swissconsin!

Why do rodents like earthquakes?
Because they like to shake, rattle, and MOLE.
From Amanda in California

What's the tallest building in the world?
The library, of course! It has the most stories.

What do you call something easy to chew?
A ch-easy chew!

From Darianne in New Hampshire

What martial art does Geronimo Stilton like to practice?
Tai Cheese!

From Ryan in Texas

What happens to a cat when it eats a lemon?
It turns into a sourpuss!

From Tiffany in Florida

How do you make a tissue dance?
You put a little boogie in it.

From Zachery in New Jersey

What do you call a group of mice in disguise?
A mouse-querade party!

From the Freed family in Michigan

How does a mouse feel after a shower?
Squeaky clean!

From Ian in Washington State

What do you call a mouse that's the size of an elephant?
Enor-mouse!

From Parker

Who was the first cat to come to America?
Christo-fur Colum-puss!

From Nora in Virginia

What's black and white and red all over?
The Rodent's Gazette! It's READ all over.

ABOUT THE AUTHOR

Born in New Mouse City, Mouse Island, Geronimo Stilton is Rattus Emeritus of Mousomorphic Literature and of Neo-Ratonic Comparative Philosophy. For the past twenty years, he has been running *The Rodent's Gazette*, New Mouse City's most widely read daily newspaper.

Stilton was awarded the Ratitzer Prize for his scoop on *The Curse of the Cheese Pyramid*. He has also received the Andersen 2000 Prize for Personality of the Year. One of his best-sellers won the 2002 eBook Award for world's best ratlings' electronic book. His works have been published all over the globe.

In his spare time, Mr. Stilton collects antique cheese rinds and plays golf. But what he most enjoys is telling stories to his nephew Benjamin.

The Rodent's Gazette

1. **Main Entrance**

2. **Printing presses (where the books and newspaper are printed)**

3. **Accounts department**

4. **Editorial room (where the editors, illustrators, and designers work)**

5. **Geronimo Stilton's office**

6. **Storage space for Geronimo's books**

Don't miss any of my other fabumouse adventures!

#1 Lost Treasure of the Emerald Eye

#2 The Curse of the Cheese Pyramid

#3 Cat and Mouse in a Haunted House

#4 I'm Too Fond of My Fur!

#5 Four Mice Deep in the Jungle

#6 Paws Off, Cheddarface!

#7 Red Pizzas for a Blue Count

#8 Attack of the Bandit Cats

#9 A Fabumouse Vacation for Geronimo

#10 All Because of a Cup of Coffee

#11 It's Halloween, You Fraidy Mouse!

#12 Merry Christmas, Geronimo!

#13 The Phantom of the Subway

#14 The Temple of the Ruby of Fire

#15 The Mona Mousa Code

#16 A Cheese-Colored Camper

#17 Watch Your Whiskers, Stilton

#18 Shipwreck on the Pirate Islands

#19 My Name Is Stilton, Geronimo Stilton

#20 Surf's Up, Geronimo

#21 The Wild, Wild West

and coming soon

A Christmas Tale

Map of New Mouse City

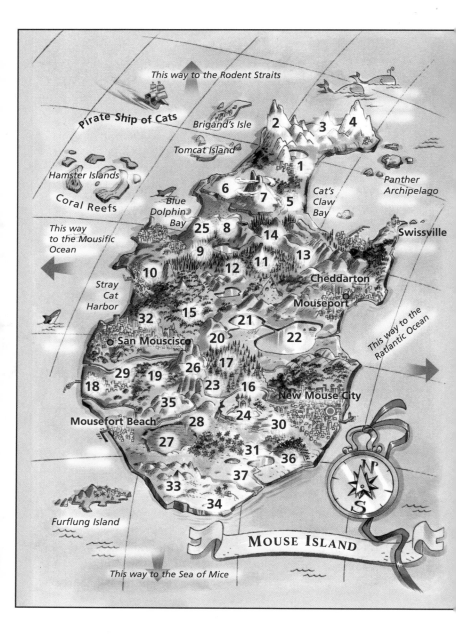

Map of Mouse Island

1. Big Ice Lake
2. Frozen Fur Peak
3. Slipperyslopes Glacier
4. Coldcreeps Peak
5. Ratzikistan
6. Transratania
7. Mount Vamp
8. Roastedrat Volcano
9. Brimstone Lake
10. Poopedcat Pass
11. Stinko Peak
12. Dark Forest
13. Vain Vampires Valley
14. Goose Bumps Gorge
15. The Shadow Line Pass
16. Penny Pincher Lodge
17. Nature Reserve Park
18. Las Ratayas Marinas
19. Fossil Forest
20. Lake Lake
21. Lake Lake Lake
22. Lake Lakelakelake
23. Cheddar Crag
24. Cannycat Castle
25. Valley of the Giant Sequoia
26. Cheddar Springs
27. Sulfurous Swamp
28. Old Reliable Geyser
29. Vole Vale
30. Ravingrat Ravine
31. Gnat Marshes
32. Munster Highlands
33. Mousehara Desert
34. Oasis of the Sweaty Camel
35. Cabbagehead Hill
36. Rattytrap Jungle
37. Rio Mosquito

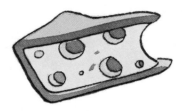

Dear mouse friends,
Thanks for reading, and farewell
till the next book.
It'll be another whisker-licking-good
adventure, and that's a promise!

Geronimo Stilton